For my good friends John and Helen
(and William, Bridget and Leo)
MD

For Emma O'Neill
Thanks to Mark, Lewis and Charlie and a debt
of gratitude to Philip, David and Eileen Pryce
at Cefn Saeson Fawr Farm in Neath
AR

SIMON AND SCHUSTER
First published in Great Britain in 2002 by Simon and Schuster UK Ltd
Africa House, 64-78 Kingsway, London, WC2B 6AH
A CBS COMPANY

This paperback edition published in 2003

A CIP catalogue record for this book is available from the British Library upon request

ISBN: 978 0 74346 215 0

Printed in China

5 7 9 10 8 6 4

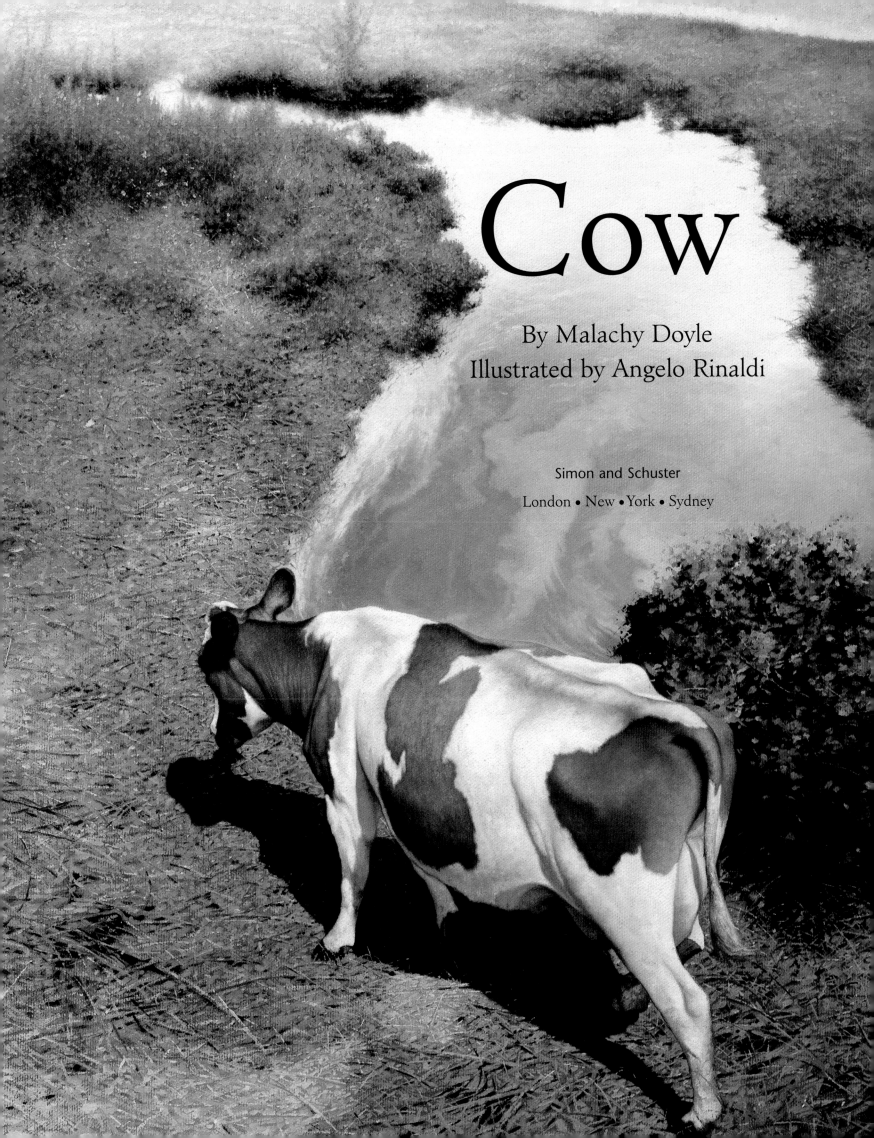

Cow

By Malachy Doyle

Illustrated by Angelo Rinaldi

Simon and Schuster

London • New •York • Sydney

Cow.

Grazing in the field on a hot summer's day.

Early morning.
Dawn is breaking.
The first birds sing,
and the farmer strolls down the lane,

whistling.

Slowly you rise from the sodden grass,
your thick coat wet with morning dew.
Big and heavy,
you amble to the gate,
full udder swinging between your legs.

Past the sheep, resting in their field,
the pigs, dozing in their pens,

the gander, keeping guard,
and the farmhouse, where the children sleep.

Your hooves click on the floor of the yard,
the gate opens and you enter the stall.

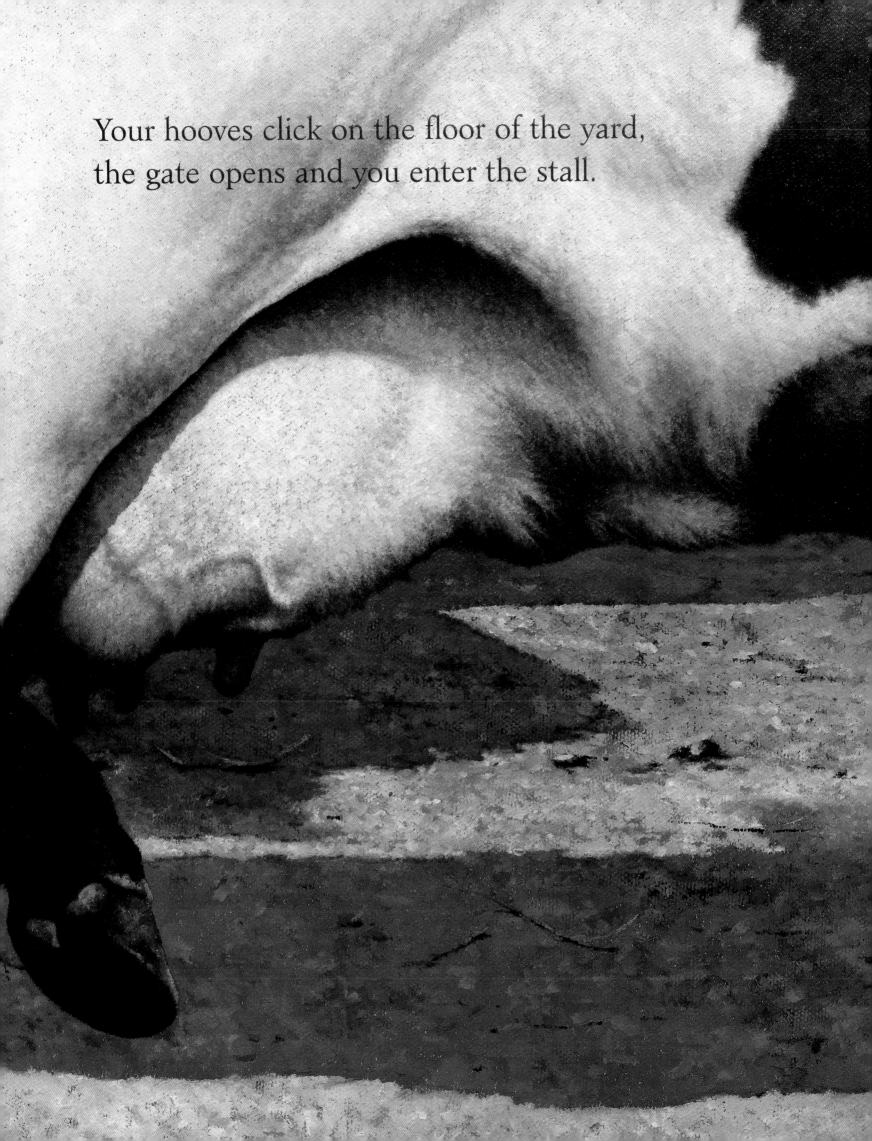

Food drops in front of you
and you bend to eat.
Gently the farmer cleans your udder,
and puts tubes on your teats.
Milk is sucked out, rich, warm,
creamy milk.

Then you wander back to the field.
Past the house, where the children are rising.
Past the coop, where the chickens are laying.

You tear the grass and chew the cud,
rolling your mouth from side to side.
Pushing the food with your thick, wet tongue,
over and over
for hours.

The school bus comes for the children,
the tanker arrives for the milk,
and slowly the morning passes.

The day warms up,
and your breath comes hot and heavy
from your broad wet nose.

You wander down to the river,
and take a long drink of the cool, clear water.

As the midday sun blazes,
you rest in the shade of the oak tree,
and close your deep, dark, eyes.
Your ears twitch to clear the flies from your face.
You swish them from your back with a long bushy tail.

The hot afternoon drags on, and the bus returns.
The children come to swing from the tree.
Out over the river,

and - splash! -

into the river.

Later you wait by the gate,
to be first in line,
your milk-full udder aching.

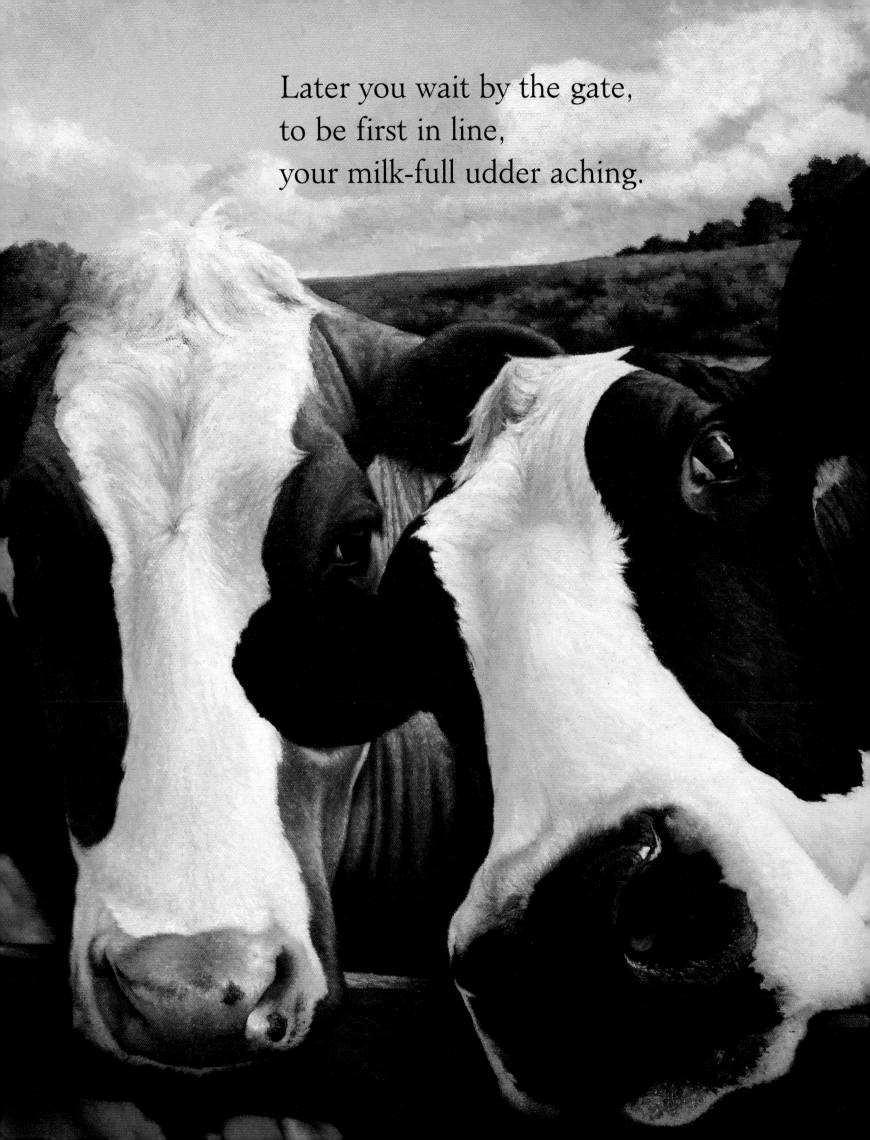

Lowing deeply as the farmer appears.

Pressing forward to the cool parlour at last.

You're back in the field.
The sun has gone.
The flies have flown,
and the long, hot day draws to an end.

You graze,

you chew,

and you rest.

It's hard work
being a cow.

Malachy Doyle is an award-winning children's writer. He lives in North Wales with his family. In *Cow* he combines a lyrical text with a wealth of information about country life. It will appeal to children of all ages, to those who already love cows and to those who live in towns and rarely see them. He has also written *Storm Cats*, illustrated by Stuart Trotter.

Angelo Rinaldi has illustrated several picture books for children. He grew up in Wales with his Italian father, Welsh mother and seven brothers and sisters, and now lives in London.

His style is highly accomplished and, in this book, he paints, using oil on canvas, the most life-evoking scenes. His landscapes breathe. You can feel the dew in the morning, see the hot air dancing at midday and relax in the cool glow of the early evening light - just like the star of the story. Cow looks real enough to touch. You can feel her warmth, hear her chew, follow her leisurely walk to the milking parlour.